TAYLOR'S BIRTHDAY PARTY

By Hana Khan

Illustrated by Mai S. Kemble

red cygnet® PRESS

San Diego, California

red cygnet® PRESS

To my family & to my teachers: For inspiring and encouraging me to always do my best.—H.K.

To Kiki, Maya, and Eva; and to Mr. Eich, thank you for being a great teach, a smart advisor, and a good friend.—M.S.K.

Illustrations copyright © 2008 Mai S. Kemble
Manuscript copyright © 2008 Hana Khan
Book copyright © 2008 Red Cygnet Press, Inc., 11858 Stoney Peak Dr. #525, San Diego, CA 92128

Cover and book design: Amy Stirnkorb

First Edition 2008
10 9 8 7 6 5 4 3 2
Printed in China

Library of Congress Cataloging-in-Publication Data

Khan, Hana.
Taylor's birthday party / written by Hana Khan ; illustrated by Mai S. Kemble. -- 1st ed.
p. cm.
Summary: Baker wants to create a surprise party for his friend Taylor, but when everything seems to be going wrong, he asks for help from friends, only to realize that it is the effort not the results that count.
ISBN-13: 978-1-60108-048-6 (hardcover)
ISBN-10: 1-60108-048-4 (hardcover)
[1. Cats--Fiction. 2. Birthdays--Fiction. 3. Parties--Fiction. 4. Friendship--Fiction.] I. Kemble, Mai S., ill. II. Title.
PZ7.K526495Tay 2008
[E]--dc22
2008015679

It was the day before Taylor's birthday.
Baker decided to surprise his best friend with a birthday party.

Baker wanted to begin by baking a cake. But, when he took out the eggs he slipped on some milk he had spilled. The eggs plopped on his head. "Oh, no!!" Baker meowed "I've got eggs in my whiskers!

Baker took out the rest of the ingredients and put them on the counter. He got more eggs from the refrigerator and put everything in a bowl. But, when Baker pressed the button to turn the mixer on, the cake batter sprayed all over the kitchen! The cake-baking was not going very well.

Baker needed to get supplies
for the party, so he rode his bike
to his favorite store: Party Pets.
At the store, Baker found some
beautiful paper lanterns. One
was a special "Happy Birthday"
lantern with monkeys on it.

Baker took the lanterns to the cashier, but there was trouble.

When he reached for them, Baker's sharp claws ripped them all! "Me and my sharp claws!" frowned Baker. He had to buy them, so he left the store with a bag of shredded paper lanterns.

After the party store, Baker went looking for a present. He spent two hours searching, but nothing seemed right. Then he found a store with glass animals! The shiny golden goldfish looked the prettiest. "That's perfect! It's Taylor's favorite animal!" Baker yelled.

He paid for the goldfish and headed home.

Baker thought it would be fun to have a few friends over for the party. He invited Robbie the rabbit, Molee the mole, Chicky the chicken, and Poky the porcupine.

He told them all about the things that had gone wrong already. Baker explained that he really wanted the party to be a surprise. The friends agreed to meet up at Baker's house at 4 p.m. the next day.

At 4 p.m. the next day, everyone set right to work. Robbie said, "To bake a cake right now, you need to be very fast. Nobody can bake a cake faster than me. So I should bake it." Poky, Molee, and Chicky nodded. "Alright," agreed Baker, "Robbie will bake the cake."

Poky whined, "I want to do something, too. Can I blow up the balloons? Nobody has as much breath as me."

"Alright," Baker declared, Poky will blow up the balloons!"

Then Molee spoke up, "I'll wrap the glass goldfish. And I'll be very careful with it since it is delicate."

"Okay," said Baker, "Molee will wrap the glass goldfish."

"And what about me?" cried Chicky.

"Chicky, you watch for Taylor. He always comes by around this time. Give a yell when you see him so we can hide."

Chicky took his place at the window and began to stand guard.

Soon, everyone was busy, but before long, everybody was complaining!

Robbie shouted, "Baker, I can't do it! It takes so much patience to bake a cake and I just can't wait!"

Before Baker could say anything, Poky complained. "And *my* sharp quills keep poking the balloons and I'm afraid they have all popped!"

Then Molee began to whimper. "I can barely see this glass goldfish because my eyes are so bad." And just then, Molee turned around and s tail knocked the goldfish over. It broke into a zillion pieces. "Oh, no!" aker cried, "Taylor will be here any minute!"

Suddenly, Chicky yelled, "Taylor's coming!"

Everybody hid. Then, as Taylor walked into the house, everybody yelled, "SURPRISE!" Taylor was shocked.

Baker walked over to his friend, holding a bowl. As he walked, he made brown mucky paw prints on the floor. "It was supposed to be your favorite milk-chocolate-chip deluxe cheesecake. It got messed up, though. Please don't be mad!"

Taylor looked at Baker and said, "Why would I be mad? You know I love to lick the bowl anyway!"

Then Poky held up a handful of popped balloons.

"They were your favorite," said Baker. "Red, blue, green, and orange."

"It was very nice of you to pick my favorite colors," said Taylor.

Taylor noticed a string of things hanging from the ceiling. "And what are those?" he asked.

"Oh," Baker answered. "Those are the paper lanterns I bought at the party store. I know how you love paper lanterns. But I'm afraid my sharp claws just ripped them all to pieces."

"Oh, that's okay," Taylor smiled. "I think they still look great."

Then, Molee and Baker held up a box and opened it. They showed Taylor the taped up goldfish.

"I'm sorry," Baker said sadly. "We accidentally broke the fish and, when we tried to wrap it, the tape kept sticking to my fur. It was supposed to be your favorite animal— a goldfish." Taylor replied, "It is very special and very pretty. And you did all this work for me? This is the best birthday ever!"

"Really?" asked Baker.

"Yes, really," Taylor smiled. "It's not about the cake, or the balloons, or presents. It's really because of all your hard work. Only good friends would do that. Thank you for making me feel so special!"

Soon it was time for the other presents. Molee gave Taylor a new video game. Poky gave him a magic trick set. Chicky gave him a board game called, "Trouble." Robbie gave him a pogo stick.

Taylor loved every one of the presents. And he loved all his friends. It had turned out to be a great party after all!